LOST IN
THE WOODS

Steve Barlow and Steve Skidmore

Illustrated by Alex Lopez

LONDON·SYDNEY

Franklin Watts
First published in Great Britain in 2016 by The Watts Publishing Group

Credits
Series Editor: Adrian Cole
Design Manager: Peter Scoulding
Cover Designer: Cathryn Gilbert
Illustrations: Alex Lopez

HB ISBN 978 1 4451 4378 1
PB ISBN 978 1 4451 4380 4
Library ebook ISBN 978 1 4451 4379 8

Printed in China.

MIX
Paper from
responsible sources
FSC® C104740

FSC
www.fsc.org

Franklin Watts
An imprint of
Hachette Children's Group
Part of The Watts Publishing Group
Carmelite House
50 Victoria Embankment
London EC4Y 0DZ

An Hachette UK Company
www.hachette.co.uk

www.franklinwatts.co.uk

Lin

Danny

Sam

The team sets off. It is soon
in trouble. "Hey! Are you sure
this is the right way?" Lin asked.

"I think we're lost," said Danny.

"What makes you say that?" asked Lin.

"I wonder what the red flag is for,"

said Danny.

"Don't worry," said Britney.

"The way back is over this fence. I think."

"Do you know where we're going?"
asked Britney.

Sam grinned. "Oh, yes."

"How?" asked Britney.

"Lin is up ahead," Sam told her.

"She's finding the way back.

We just have to follow her..."

"This way!" said Lin.

"Thank goodness!" said Mr Broad.

"Where have you been?"

"It was them, sir!" said Clogger Mills.

"The freaks. They got us lost!"

"And shot at!" Britney added.